To that very special beast, The Mongee

A CIP record of this book is available from the British Library
Text and illustrations © 1993 Diz Wallis
First published in the United Kingdom 1993 by
Ragged Bears Limited,Ragged Appleshaw,
Andover, Hampshire SP11 9HX
ALL RIGHTS RESERVED
ISBN 1 85714 034 6
Printed in Singapore

Based on the Grimms' tale *The Willow Wren and the Bear*

BATTLE OF THE BEASTS

Written and illustrated by

DIZ WALLIS

RAGGED BEARS

D id you know, it was once said, the tiny wren was the King of Birds? Now Bear, who had heard this tale, was sitting by a pond when a wren flew out from some reeds nearby. He was filled with curiosity and whispered to his friend, "Let's go and find his palace, for I've never seen one yet. We'll inspect the royal quarters while the King's away." But the wolf was embarrassed and hung back.

Bear pulled away the hanging willow and drew aside the swaying sedge, until he saw the tiny palace and its princely contents. He laughed, "Five puny little birdies in a nasty little nesty, with a scrubby, shrubby garden all around. Why, you're no more royal than I am. You're very humble offspring, I would say."

The princelings were furious. "You furry old fool! Common creature from the woods," they shrieked, "bend your shabby, shaggy knees and apologise at once." But Bear wouldn't. He laughed at them. He was really very rude.

When the wren returned he found the nest in uproar. "Can't sleep. Won't eat. Take that worm away," yelled the cross little birds, "won't talk to you at all until that bear is punished and says sorry." The wren was so distressed when he heard what had happened, he went to Bear and said, "Kneel down before the princelings and apologise at once."

"What! Grovel to some pipsqueaks in a scruffy old nesty?" said Bear, "I'll do no such thing. In this world, I assure you, it's the lion who's King and I'll bend these shabby, shaggy knees to no one else!"

T hen it's war," cried the tiny wren. "We'll teach you some respect! It's the fur against the feather. Creatures who are earth-bound against all those that fly." But Bear just scoffed and walked away. Though at the bottom of his heart he felt uneasy. Had he gone too far? Might this wren be really royal?

Now the birds got together and they formed a great council. There was twittering and tweeting, chirping and cheeping, and a raucous squawking from some slick, black crows. They were cross, very cross when they heard the little wren speak.

How dare this great and grizzly oaf of a bear insult the little princelings in the way he had? There was no doubt about it, there was going to be a battle, that was sure.

Then the beasts got together; they came from far and wide. There was howling and growling, braying and barking and a chorus of grunting from a herd of spotted pigs. They were cross, very cross. How dare this little wren and its itsy-bitsy nestlings that could fit inside a nutshell, assume such airs and graces? They must be taught a lesson. There was going to be a battle, that was sure.

The hare told the weasels, and the weasels told the stoats, and who knows who the stoats told, but from snout to snout and beak to beak the message passed. It was not long before the word spread across the world.

All creatures were called on to decide which side their loyalties lay. Even insects were expected to attend. They buzzed and they hummed but they stopped what they were doing and set out for the battlefield at once.

S oon frogs and toads crept from their crevices, mostly travelling at night for fear the sun might scorch their skins. Moths made their way by moonlight along with fire-flies and nightingales, to mention but a few. The o-o and the dodo and the noisy friar bird went too, with moonrats and numbats and leaping kangaroos.

The camel left the desert, the leopard left his dappled jungle. Monkeys ceased to play in the forest canopy. Spoonbills and ibises vacated the mangrove swamps. They were off to join the battle as fast as they could go, alongside skunks and armadillos and an ancient, giant tortoise who is going still.

A lmost all the creatures of the earth that could walk or crawl or fly set out to join their side, though there were a few exceptions; the cats, for one, refused to go, for they are contrary types and never, ever like to oblige. Besides, the days were warm and they were tired.

And in the squelchy puddles by the muddy Mississippi, a great, squat, knobbly 'gator received the message and the messenger. He snapped his jaws and mused, "I would go, if I could go, but I must digest the news."

Then he flicked his tail and smiled and slipped back into the bayou and floated there a while.

The night before the battle, the troops assembled. The birds made up their minds to send a spy into the rivals' camp. They chose the gnat. She hid beneath the dark leaves where the moonlight could not reach. The noise was tremendous; some of the troops were sleeping, and it was difficult to hear above the snores and the snorts. But concealed in the shadows the gnat listened hard.

The fox and the lion and the bear sat in a huddle. "I," said the fox, "will lead the army into battle, riding on the elephant, so that all the troops will see me. My brush will be our standard and as long as it is raised we can advance, but if I let it drop, then you'll know we've been defeated and we must retreat."

The gnat returned and reported what was said. Soon the birds hatched a plan. They would use their secret weapon... they would send in the hornet. All night long she sharpened up her sting. She buffed and she honed, until it was needle keen and glinted in the moonlight like a highly polished skewer. It was a very deadly weapon indeed!

By the time dawn broke, preparations were complete. The birds were preened to perfection with not a feather out of place. They assembled into squadrons that were glorious to see. There was booming and cooing, warbling and whistling and the sky grew dark with wings.

T he noise woke up the bear, who shook himself and cried, "Get ready to do battle, beasts, form into a rabble fast." So they stretched and scratched and yawned and they got themselves together in a raggle-taggle way.

Then the fox tried to climb onto the elephant's back. It was quite a sight to see, but he managed in the end and he led the troops forward with his tail held high.

The birds advanced too, but their highly painted plumage was lost behind the dust raised by padded paw and hoof.

T he hornet flew up and closed in upon her target and delivered her sting to the fox's rump. Once and twice she stung and the brush began to quiver. On the third strike, with a yowl, the tail dropped down.

When the four-footed beasts saw their standard lowered they cried "Oh! We're injured! Oh! We're dying!" And they fled across the field for the shelter of the forest. Then they searched through their fur to look for wounds, but all they could find was some badly hurt pride and one very sore behind.

Poor old Bear, he felt so dejected as he waited for his punishment, for the mocking birds mocked him and the laughing kookaburras chuckled from the trees, but his greatest irritation was the sound of someone sniggering in the 'possum's pouch.

Soon the wren flew in and settled by Bear, whose head hung low in shame. "Well, you old fool, it seems the 'four-foots' were routed. I hope you've learned your lesson and gained some respect! Now," piped the little bird, "go to the princelings and apologise and make sure you show them all the honour they deserve."

O h! What indignity. Oh! What a spectacle. The birds and the beasts all craned their necks to watch the show as Bear knelt before the nestlings and said, "Please forgive your humble servant. You are really royal highnesses, and your father is a king, while I am just a stupid old bear, a furry old fool from the woods."

The chicks were thankful for they were feeling very hungry, so ignoring the apology, they opened wide their beaks and shrieked "FOOD!"

Now the argument was over and life returned to normal.
The animals went back to their faraway homes. In the end,
Bear got over his deep humiliation, but he always avoided those little brown birds.